Tales
of the
Old Mariner

Tales
of the
Old Mariner

Akin Fatimehin

AMVPS

Published by
AMV Publishing Services
259 Nassau Street Ste 2 #661
Princeton NJ 08542-4609
Tel: + 1 609-627-9168 - Fax: + 1 609-716-7224
emails: publisher@amvpublishingservices.com &
customerservice@amvpublishingservices.com
worldwide web: https://amvpublishingservices.com

Tales of the Old Mariner

This is a work of fiction. Names, characters, places, and incidents either are the product of the author's imagination or are used fictitiously. Any likeness or resemblance to actual persons, living or dead, events, or locales is entirely coincidental.

Copyright © 2022 Akin Fatimehin

All rights reserved. No part of this publication may be reproduced, stored in a retrieval system, or transmitted in any form or by any means, electronic, mechanical, photocopying, recording or otherwise without the written permission of the publisher.

Book & Cover Design: AMV Origination & Design Division

Library of Congress Control Number: 2021940137

ISBN: 978-978-965-339-3

CHAPTER 1

THE MARINER'S MAN

These tales were told by the man generally known as "the Mariner". In the district where we lived as kids, that was the name which everybody seemed to call him, although his real name was Kelvin.

Legend had it that he worked on a ship for a long period of his life. It was said that he had been to many countries, travelled many islands, and sailed across many seas. They said he was a rugged seaman.

Nothing appeared rugged about this gentleman who always sat at the baobab tree base surrounded by we kids. He was in between his late fifties and early sixties, with a mass of grey hair and a slim but tall frame.

Everyday, except Sundays, he spent a couple of hours with us kids regaling us with tales of his adventurous days. He usually left us early evening for more adult company at the local beer parlour where, I guess, he did the same thing with the adults. Yet he was more or less a loner, this old sailor. He was good company, but looking back on it, one sensed aloofness in him. This sailor was a friend of the seas. Water, limitless horizons of water would always be his companion. No amount of land would do. And no amount of its occupants for that matter. Was this why he still had no offspring with his thirty-something years of age wife — a stunning beauty with hazel eyes and a natural light complexioned woman called Martha.

The Mariner had married late and for reasons no one seemed to know, had not sired an offspring. But do not let us get too way ahead of our tale.

It was from the Mariner that we kids in the district first learnt the names of the various islands — Panama, Tupamaru and Falklands. Strange sounding names, yet sweet to the ears.

We nicknamed ourselves after these islands. I was Arabella; T.J. was Panama; Ahmed was Tupamaru, but does that really have a bearing to the tale? We also learnt traditional modes of greetings amongst sea men from him. Ahoy, Ahoa, Alora, First mate, Deckhand... all the works... God it was fun!

Anyway much of this first story is not about the Old Mariner, but about some incident which occurred that served to shape the lives of many of us who were beneficiaries of his tales.

I said earlier that each day, especially during holidays, many children in the neighbourhood, and some from as far as the district border, would converge under the baobab tree when we would be regaled by the Mariner with tales of some ancient or far away island.

This day it had been some tale about Falklands which the Mariner had not been able to finish before he dashed down to the local beer parlour. He had promised us that he would complete the tale the following day, and so eagerly, we waited the next day. But alas we were at the baobab's base as early as we could muster and yet the old Mariner was not there. This was unprecedented. The Mariner had never failed to keep his promise.

We went to his house, his usual local beer parlour and every other place where we felt he could be. But no dice. The Mariner was no where to be found. After what seemed like eternity, we all gave up. We were dejected but equally prayerful that nothing terrible had happened to the Old Mariner. Our Old Mariner.

As dusk approached, we got news that the Mariner had been sighted. Quickly we gathered ourselves and proceeded to the location — another local beer parlour, different from the one he usually frequented. And then we saw the reason. He had company.

It was an elderly man about the same age with the Mariner. He had grayish hair too. But a black well trimmed goatee. We could see from where we stood with our young excited eyes that he wore a white, well-starched shirt, grey slacks and a maroon-coloured tie.

The Mariner spotted us as we waved to him, excited. In those days, youngsters were not allowed into local beer parlours. He came out to meet us, the usual glint in his eyes, as was the case whenever he saw us.

"Home boys, home," he bellowed, in his baritone voice. "Tomorrow we'll meet beneath the baobab and I'll tell you what all this is about."

I know most of us hardly slept the night as the excitement was too much. Who was this stranger who spoke so animatedly with our dear Old Mariner, we all asked ourselves. What did he want? What had he come to tell him? Was the Mariner going again on a long extended journey?

D-Day came and yes, we all rushed to the baobab's base and it was there that the Mariner told us all what we longed to hear. It wasn't the tale of a far flung island or archipelago. It was the story of his friend. The very one who had come to see him the previous day. It is that story that I christened the Mariner's friend, "The Mariner's Man."

"My Man," the Mariner had called him. "My Main Man; just as you are kids now, we were kids together. His name is Alfred. In the same village we grew up, attending the same school we were not only school mates. We were soul mates."

Many pranks they had played together, the Mariner and his Main Man, Alfred. He remembered a few of them, like when they stole out of college to buy bean cakes at the college's township. On their way back they were accosted by the school principal, Mr. Johnson. Believing the principal had not seen them, they did not realise that the cat had been let out of the bag.

The Mariner, on that fateful night, had been wearing the school's football jersey with number 22 boldly inscribed at the back. After prayers and announcement at the assembly, Mr Johnson had called out, "Who is in possession of the school's football jersey, number 22?"

The Mariner had calmly stepped out not knowing what was amiss.

"Where were you last night at 10:00pm?" queried the principal.

That was how the cat had been let out of the bag, and the Mariner and his accomplice had received 22 strokes of the cane. Many other such pranks, the Mariner told us about on this fateful evening.

Years after, the Mariner and his friend had parted ways to pursue different careers. The Mariner had gone ahead to join the navy, while his Main Man Alfred, had gone to pursue a career in teaching. Yet both had remained in close contract monitoring each other's progress.

The Mariner said he understood that his Main Man was quite good at his vocation. He had the singular record in the district school where he taught as the one teacher who never laid a rod on the kids. "He had a gentle way of relating with the kids," said the Mariner. Words had a more far reaching effect on the children than even a thousand strokes would have, and his kids always did well in class. Throughout his career, he had maintained an unblemished record of never having nurtured a student who failed his course. The Mariner made us know that he had come to love kids because of the way his Main Man related to children. But that was not what his friend's visit had been all about, he told us.

Because of the nature of his vocation, the Mariner's Man had not been able to gain much in terms of materials acquisition.

Those were the days, or, are they still so now when it was often said that the teacher's reward lay in heaven.

In fact, in many instances, the Mariner's Man had been the butt of many cruel jokes amongst his contemporaries because of his indigent state.

It wasn't that he was completely forgotten by his former students, it was just that there was very little they themselves could do to salvage his overall situation.

Many of his former students had grown to become successful career men and women, and often tried to make sure that their former teacher and mentor did not lack in the very basic things of life. His furniture, feeding items and even the home in which he lived in had been provided by some of his benevolent former students.

But this only seemed to worsen his case among his contemporaries, as they soon began to call him beggar-teacher.

All this had gone on until recently when something novel happened in the district of Oyigbo, where the Mariner's Man had taught and lived all his adult life.

The new wind of democracy blowing across the nation had reached the district of Oyigbo. In the council elections held in the district, the four sons of the Mariner's man, had contested for four different positions. All four had won. Their names were Bill, John, Wilfred and Charles.

This was something unprecedented, considering the fact that the Mariner's Man was not even a native of the district. His critics were silent, the detractors went back home with their tails between the legs.

A great moral lesson had been taught. A general victory had been achieved. Those who had felt otherwise began to change their ways. The refrain was, "If you care for other people's kids, yours will most assuredly be successful."

The teacher's reward was no longer in heaven, it was right here on earth. That was the tale the Mariner told us about his Main

Man, and we were happy as we perplexed at the turn of events.

We all thought the tale had ended there until a few months later we began to notice some changes in the Mariner's wife. She became more rotund and prettier. Then she blossomed even further as she grew bigger.

It was a boy and we were all there for the naming. "Acapulco", he was named, after some other far away island.

We had all learnt a lesson from the tale of the Mariner's Man, but apparently it was the Mariner himself who learnt the biggest.

CHAPTER 2

OCEAN ELEVEN

We loved football; we all did while we were young. Even now as adults, nothing unites us more in this part of the world than football.

Childhood camaraderie cannot be complete if the sport of football is not part of the binding force. A recount of childhood experiences cannot be made without adequate mention of football. We loved it. Yes we did. And we indulged in it a lot.

In fact it seemed that as youngsters, our entire lives revolved around football. No day was complete if one had not partaken of the round leather game. Many a times, even contrary to our parents' directives, we usually sneaked out to played O.J.O; we played eleven; we played work and eat.

At a time we decided to form a district youth team and of course, we went through all the works. We found a coach, one of the P.E. teachers, Mr Patrick, in one of the district schools, and everyday at an appointed time we met for a considerable period of time until we decided to host a neighborhood district team to a friendly game.

Of course, I forgot to mention that all that time, we were too impoverished to have a standard ball which we used for practice.

Match day came and for some reason, our coach selected the first eleven and left out the boy, the owner of the ball, from the starting line.

Why didn't we pick the Old Mariner as our coach? Was it on account of his advanced years or was it because in his many stories, he had never spoken of football? No one knows, but match day came with both teams ready to do justice to the round leather game.

Crowd, referee, his assistant and all the works. But there was a snag. There was no ball to play.

The sponsor team too did not bring a ball and our friend-turned-benefactor, chose this all important day not to show up. Most likely on account of the fact that he had not made the team.

We were all very incensed. We wanted to find the culprit' and beat the brains out of him. The opposing team had left in annoyance leaving us with our disgrace. We were all wild in our rage.

It was as we stepped out of the district field, marching towards the culprit's house that we spotted the Old Mariner, smoking his pipe, as usual, under the baobab tree.

"It seems something is amiss ," he said matter-of-factly.

"A lot is the matter," we replied in

enraged unison. He asked us what had happened and we told him everything.

"You guys must be joking," he said as he burst out laughing. "You guys must be real jokes. You didn't pick the guy with the ball?" He asked, again laughing. "The guy with the ball has always got to be in the team," he said, emphasizing every word.

"Football is like real life, you know, and you have to treat it as such. I'll tell you about that later, but first of all let me tell you about a team to which I belonged while I was in the Navy."

The Old Mariner then went ahead to tell us of his football team named the "Ocean Eleven". It was a team made up of his ship's crew which was made up of exactly eleven men apart from the captain, Master Rhodes.

Since there were only eleven men, it was imperative that each man make the team. Secondly, since the team did not have the privilege of reserve players, it was imperative that each man remain fit.

Thirdly, the coach had to harness both the weaknesses and strengths of individuals into one harmony.

That was the state of things with the Ocean Eleven. There was a center-forward; the Old Mariner could only score with his head.

There was a goalkeeper who was only good at saving penalties, a left half-back who was always instructed by the coach to tackle outside box eighteen because of his rough play, and a right full-back who was left footed.

These amongst others were the oddities which characterized the Ocean Eleven.

However, the coach had been able to harness all these weaknesses and strengths into a formidable whole, a team which won more matches than it lost in the many friendly matches it played on the various islands where the team's ship berthed.

And that is the whole point the Mariner added. The whole point of life. Remember, I told you life is exactly like football.

The Mariner went on to tell us how in life, just like in football, we had to pick our "eleven". And there is never a perfect eleven; we all have to harmonize the strengths and weaknesses of those we find available to us and make it a collective workable machinery. E.g.:

— A nagging wife, but a domestic genius also good with finance.
— A miserly friend but always morally and psychologically supportive.
— A critical uncle but a financial backbone.
— An ill aunt with so much love and care to give out.

"That is what life always gives us," said the Old Mariner. "We can never ever get perfection. I would have gone ahead to say that there is no dream team in reality," he said, "but there is."

He cleared his throat and continues. "We all have the power to create our dream team. That is what coach Rhodes taught us with the Ocean Eleven, and the message has remained with me ever since," he concluded.

By the way, when next you have a match, put the guy with the ball in the first eleven.

CHAPTER 3

JUST LIKE THE MAGI

Some of us left the district. After elementary school, we had to leave for secondary school. And since boarding schools were still functional at that time, some of us had to leave the district.

Of course, we all went to different schools.

While some stayed within the district, some of us gained admission into schools outside the district. One or two of us even went as far as attending schools at neighboring cities

It was a brand new world, our first term at school. Being away from home was as exciting as it was frightening. We came in contact with several things and terms that were alien to our former world. Double Decker beds, lockers, math sets, T-squares and cricket. Yes in my own case cricket was a novelty.

This new game had its different rules as they taught about accuracy, concentration, endurance and speed. Of course we always loved to play cricket. Always wanted to play it. We had lockers as lockets, milk tins as cock balls and T-squares as bats. We played, yes we played.

And worked too. There was general assembly in the mornings, songs of praise, and prayer sessions in the chapel and mosque. Even allowance was made for free thinkers in those days.

There was childhood innocence. There was friendship. There was joy. There was pain. There was betrayal.

One of the several pranks we played was to get somebody to eavesdrop while we searched for an innocent boy to initiate a derogatory dialogue about the eaves dropper. Usually, the dialogue went like this:

Dialogue initiator: That T (eaves dropper) is such a miserly person. Yesterday I asked for cubes of sugar he refused but when I have, he is always coming to take mine.

Innocent boy: You are right, T is so miserly and greedy. Just day before yesterday....

After tricking the innocent boy into saying several derogatory things about the eavesdropper, the eavesdropper would emerge from his hide out and the innocent boy would discover a trap had been set for him. Usually we had a good laugh at his expense. Yet we regarded it as childhood pranks. No matter the amount of verbal damage done, we were always quick to forgive and forget.

How come that it was so easy to forgive and forget as youngsters? What transition occurs to our psyches that at adulthood, we nurture and keep malice and grudges? Oh that we were boys again. God! The problems of adulthood, most of which was our selective amnesia — choosing to forget some things and deliberately willing ourselves to remember others. Often times, we form the whole thing up in our heads; things we are supposed to forget, we don't, while the ones we weren't, we did.

For instance if a guy gave us a ride while we were struck in traffic, we may conveniently choose to forget about it. Ask the same guy for a coke sometime and he says "no", then we go and find a safe place in our brains to store the information.

Anyway that is a tale for adults, we are presently talking about our first holidays.

We came back home to discover that a lot had changed in the district.

There was a new political leadership in the district, and along with it, there were new physical infrastructures.

For example, our football field had been converted into a site for a new town hall. A hotel stood at the grove, where we held our youth meetings. There were now tourists in our district. White folks of different ages, sizes and sexes frequented our borders for what they termed as vacationing, and as a result, our local currency was not held in the same esteem as it used to be.

There was now a new currency making the grounds. The Dollar, they called it. Some shops even refused to collect our local currency in exchange for goods. They preferred the white man's Dollar.

What had happened to our village? We loved our district as it used to be. Now even the constant supply of electricity did not make our moonlight nights what they used to be.

But the most disturbing information we received upon our return from school was that our dear old baobab tree had to go on account of some new road that was to lead to the market square. What was this?

Where would we meet the Old Mariner for our daily dosage of resounding tales? Where would we share with him the experiences we had at school? We went to meet the Old Mariner at his home and told him how we felt about the situation; how we felt our district was being eroded. But this is what he told us.

"As a youngster, I was fascinated by the city of L, that was where I used to go and spend my holidays with my several uncles, aunties and other relative who lived and worked there.

"Life in the city of L in those days proceeded at a very leisurely yet lively pace. That was the era often regarded as the high-life years. Because the nation was still under colonial rule, foreigners sort of dominated the city. The social life consisted of visits to the various beaches and dance halls. Life in the city of L was all in all predominantly pleasant.

"I took a keen interest in literary activities. I remember taking part in some literary debates organized by colonial literary societies. I remember we used to attend political rallies and campaigns where the all time great politicians used to come and tell of their great vision for this nation.

"The cinema was a ma1or centre of attraction in the city of L. Either in couples or individually, we thronged the various cinema houses to steal a glimpse of what was going on in the outside world.

"And then I 1oined the Navy and one of my first voyages took me away for a very, very long time. I was away for several years. The voyage had taken me to very many far and distant places. I had many experiences. Saw several cultures and met many diverse peoples. But somehow, the city of L was always on my mind. I longed for the beaches and the cinema, the debates and the politics.

"All through my journey, I prayed for the day I would return to the city of L where I hoped to settle down even after my naval career.

"It was with great expectation that I returned to the city of L after my long sojourn. But alas all my hopes were dashed. First I visited the beaches and rather than meet the peace, quiet and solitude which characterized the place, it was chaos and disorderliness everywhere. It was rife with crime, prostitution and drug abuse. This typified my former haven of solace.

"And then the streets of the city of L, oh my God! Rural-urban migration had destroyed the serenity of the township. Rural dwellers thought the streets to be paved with gold. They arrived in droves to do exactly nothing. Many had even began to sleep under bridges.

"Instead of the literary activities of the days of old, what one was confronted with was a mass of paper vendors who adorned tables with junk magazines parading nude and half nude girls on their covers.

"The cinema culture had given way to home videos that celebrated voodoo and nudity as the best thing to come out of our nation.

"The good old post office, recipient of important correspondence, had given way to cyber cafes, and machines had begun to duplicate the functions of man.

"So many changes, man, too numerous to count. But the one that got to me most was the psyche of the inhabitants of the city of L. In the past, they generally took things easy, helped each other out and accepted their various status in life. Each was now out at his utmost to outwit the other in the criminality of their thoughts and actions.

"And so, I left the city of L with a vow never to return. I stay back in the district now, only going to L for reasons relating to my pension.

"And things are far worse now; they now live like criminals behind bars. Or worst still animals behind cages; each one is afraid of the other."

The Mariner paused a bit before concluding. "So you better learn life's lessons fast. Nothing stays the same. Things usually change and most times not in the ways we expect.

"Modernity, we all crave it, but when it comes...," he made a gesture with his fingers, "out of the window goes our rest of mind and valued essence."

Modernity, ask the magi.

CHAPTER 4

TO TELL OR NOT TO TELL

We grew older and as we grew older we began to be confronted with more mature issues. We also began to imbibe moral codes.

"Ten kids cannot play together for ten years," so the adage goes. Perhaps it would have been more apt to say that "ten kids will not remain kids in ten years."

Our character formation took routes which we could not begin to immediately acknowledge and articulate even as it went on. It was so subtle in form that we hardly took notice of it. Yet it went on.

We had begun our various life journeys, and the morals we imbibed as kids often pointed the direction in which those journeys would proceed.

We made friends; we subconsciously learnt that friendship — true friendship — was one of the greatest virtues which the Almighty bestowed on mankind. We fought and quarrelled yet we made up and continued. We laughed together, cried together, played pranks together, and got into trouble together.

But we were all cemented in our knowledge that we would always be there for one another, never to squeal on one another.

Of course, there were internal conflicts in our well-designed moral orientations. Sometimes our commitment to friendship was usually called to question. The question was "could we always rise to the occasion when it came to the issue of this great bestowment of God?"

One case in point went thus: we had stolen out of school to catch a film show in town. I do not remember clearly now, but I think it was about six of us. A Chinese film it was, popular in those days for its kicks and jumps, twists and turns. And we had a good time.

Night life was virtually non-existent then in the township where we schooled, since there were no taxis plying the roads then. We discovered one of the large holes in the barbed wire which fenced the entire school. In fact, we were the ones who had created the hole but that is a tale for another day. Anyway, the night guard had gone ahead to inform the school principal that he had spotted some boys sneaking out of school in that dead of night.

As we came back and were about to go in through the same hole, the first one to do so fell right into waiting hands of the school principal. He was a smart fellow, that one. As soon as he saw that he had been apprehended, he let out a loud yell to let us know that danger was at hand.

We all took to our heels even as we sought out other well-known alternative routes that let us into the school and fast to the safety of our beds before the principal could decide to take a general roll call. But he didn't do that. What he did was summon an assembly. The boy's name was Leke. The principal then went ahead and presented Leke with two options.

After announcing the "grave" crime which the boy had been caught committing, Leke was told to either call out the names of his fellow culprits and be allowed to go without punishment or he should receive twenty four of the school principal's lethal strokes.

There was pin drop silence as the whole school assembly and we fellow culprits waited with bated breath for the boy's decision.

Proudly he stepped toward the principal, pointing out his left arm thus signifying that he preferred to take the strokes in his hand rather than the buttocks. The whole assembly burst out in applause.

As children, we never learnt our lessons. We were off to catch another film show. Again we were apprehended. This time it was I who was apprehended. The school principal did give me the choice that Leke got me. I shall either name the other boys that went out with me or go on suspension and miss school for the whole term. I didn't need any prodding to make my decision. I took the suspension.

And so I had come home and told the tale to everyone who cared to listen and everyone, except my father who refused to say anything, had blamed me for my decision. The suspension is different from 24 strokes of the cane. You know what missing a term can do to your educational career, people said, you may end up losing one whole year! Since my father didn't say anything, I went to the Old Mariner, our alternate father, and this is what he said.

"In life we are all always confronted with choices; we always have to make choices in order to forge ahead. Sometimes there is a big dividing line between the things that confront us, and making a decision is not a problem.

"But at other times, the moral divide is so thin that making what would amount to a decision becomes a big difficulty. One big man I know once said that he would rather take a wrong decision than not take any decision at all. But even that may be a bit beside the point.

"Societies, clubs, and fraternities, all have codes of secrecy. In the pursuance of virtue, to bond and cement friendships, men are not called upon to squeal on their friends. I am not talking about the rubbish cults that abound these days. Those ones will go and cause trouble over some trivial issues, like a contested girlfriend, and then pay lip service to a code of silence. They lie. They know nothing of virtue. They know nothing of camaraderie. Check it out boy. Check it out. If apprehended by the authorities, they are the first to start singing like a canary.

"What you did was right, my boy. You stood by your friends by demonstrating a moral virtue. Just like the first boy had done. You told me he received applause by the student body for his decision. You deserve an award. And you will get it.

"Someday, in the near or far future, one of those other boys will remember your act of friendship and courage, and he will call you to a position of responsibility. Mark my words boy. Mark them. Now run along and catch your fun. I'll see you some other time.

CHAPTER 5

ASCENDING THE DECKS

We grew up more and left college. Oh what an experience! Final exams, send of parties, valedictory service, and freedom at last. It was time to go to the university. The ultimate arrival in the world of adults.

Competition was very high in those days and to get admission into universities or polytechnics was seen as the height of achievement for our levels.

It was a case of serious swatting and endless nights of burning the midnight oil for the matriculation examinations which almost always coincided with our final examinations.

I got in; three other boys in the district also got admission — we were the only lucky ones in our entire district. It was celebration galore, at both individual and collective levels. We were all so very glad. But getting into the university was one thing, staying in was another. The university culture was totally unprecedented. Here, we were confronted with unlimited freedom. It was a total contrast to the regimentation and strictness we had encountered in our various colleges.

Even if one chose, he could refuse to attend lectures. And there were the clubs, the fraternities; the parties too were there to lure you. My friends and I proposed within us to outdo everyone in what they seemed to know how to do best — socializing.

And then there were girls, plenty of them. And because there were girls, there was love, lust and infatuation, and many other categories which fell between. It was all in the air.

In this kind of atmosphere, it was difficult for a young local district boy like me not to fall victim. Many of us lost our heads and became victims of the partying and notorious living. Before we knew it, exams were at the door. It was too late to effect any major rectification. At the end of the year, I had to repeat the class.

I went back home discouraged and dejected. I believed I had turned myself into the district's laughing stock. I believed I had misused the great opportunity given to me. I believed I had breached the high trust placed on me. I was further dejected because I learnt that some of my mates who hadn't made it to the university the previous year were making fun of me. Their envy had turned into gladness because they believed they had finally caught up with me. It was sad because I hadn't seen it that way.

In fact when I was home for the semester vacation, I tried to carry everybody along and made sure not to snub anyone. I felt deeply hurt when I heard that some of my friends had misconstrued the tales of the university which I regaled them with as an attempt at being pompous.

Thus it was that I withdrew into a shell. I engaged in little socializing and I shunned many of the places where I believed I could run into any of these boys or indeed any other boy.

I also didn't go to the Mariner, despite the fact that boys my age mate still went to see him for daily dosages of rib crackling humour and elderly wit and wisdom. So it was big surprise when one day, close to the end of the vacation, the Mariner came to look for me.

My father had come into my room as I lay listening to Bob Marley's *Who the Cap Fits,* to tell me I had a visitor.

Surprise etched on my face as I encountered the Old Mariner sitting casually on my father's favorite couch, puffing away at his trademark pipe.

"I hear you didn't make it boy," he bellowed. "I asked around with other boys and they said you have not been coming around because you didn't make it. The race is not for the swift, you know?" He stopped. Then continued. "It is for those who can endure. And we are not talking some hundred meters race here. We are talking of some long distance race, which is what the race of life is all about. Are you getting me?" he asked.

"Yes sir," I replied.

"Don't let any damn Geography teacher fool you by saying that the higher you go, the cooler it becomes. Boy the hotter it gets." He stopped. Refilled his pipe which had gone out, then continued.

"In the race of life, boy, there are pitfalls, and the whole place is littered with potholes. There are those who will despise you for no just reason, and there are those who will loathe and hate you. There are those who will be jealous of you. There are those who will be envious of you and not wish you well. But you just don't let all these bother you. There will always be those who love you and wish you well, no matter how rough the going gets. There will always be at least someone there for you, even if it appears that there is none. Always remember the big guy up there. He is always looking out for you," he concluded.

****

Needless to say, I went back to school and smashed the exams to smithereens. Not only that, I went ahead to top the graduating class of my department.

And yes, the rest as they say, is history.

www.ingramcontent.com/pod-product-compliance
Lightning Source LLC
LaVergne TN
LVHW041559070526
838199LV00046B/2046